Five reasons why we think you'll love this bo[ok]

Winnie AND Wilbur
IN SPACE

This book will take you into space!

Winnie turns one of her turrets into a rocket.

There is so much to spot in every picture.

You're just going to love the space rabbits.

You can ... ... ur challenge: can you ... ... solar system?

Freya

Anushka

Maggie

Bailey

Johannes

Molly

Ashley

Amber

Jun-Yeong

Pablo

Matilda

Marwin

Hasan

Rebecca

Thank you to all these schools for helping with the endpapers:

St Barnabas Primary School, Oxford; St Ebbe's Primary
School, Oxford; Marcham Primary School, Abingdon; St
Michael's C.E. Aided Primary School, Oxford; St Bede's
RC Primary School, Jarrow; The Western Academy, Beijing,
China; John King School, Pinxton; Neston Primary School,
Neston; Star of the Sea RC Primary School, Whitley Bay;
José Jorge Letria Primary School, Cascais, Portugal; Dunmore
Primary School, Abingdon; Özel Bahçeşehir İlköğretim Okulu,
Istanbul, Turkey; the International School of Amsterdam, the
Netherlands; Princethorpe Infant School, Birmingham.

For Helen Mortimer—V.T.

For Molly Dallas—K.P

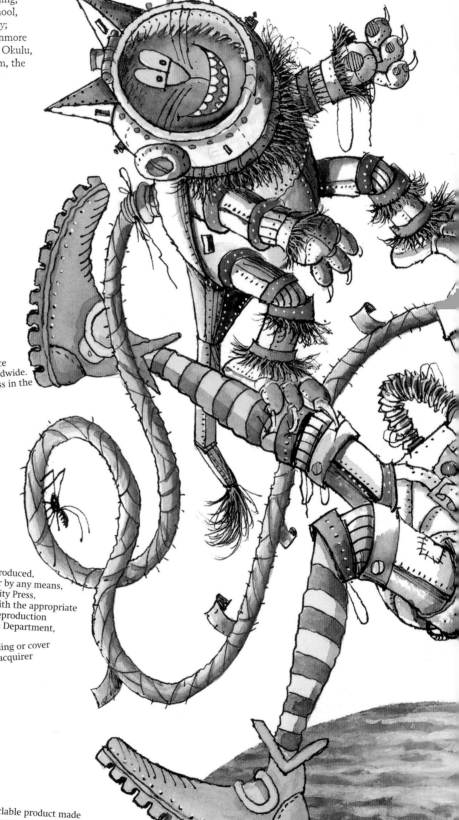

OXFORD
UNIVERSITY PRESS

Great Clarendon Street, Oxford OX2 6DP

Oxford University Press is a department of the University
of Oxford. It furthers the University's objective of excellence
in research, scholarship, and education by publishing worldwide.
Oxford is a registered trade mark of Oxford University Press in the
UK and in certain other countries

Text copyright © Valerie Thomas 2010
Illustrations copyright © Korky Paul 2010, 2016
The moral rights of the author and artist
have been asserted

Database right Oxford University Press (maker)

First published as *Winnie in Space* in 2010

This edition first published in 2016

British Library Cataloguing in Publication Data available

ISBN: 978-0-19-274825-6 (paperback)
ISBN: 978-0-19-274915-4 (paperback and CD)

10 9 8 7 6 5 4

Printed in China

Paper used in the production of this book is a natural, recyclable product made
from wood grown in sustainable forests. The manufacturing process conforms
to the environmental regulations of the country of origin

www.winnieandwilbur.com

VALERIE THOMAS AND KORKY PAUL

Winnie and Wilbur
IN SPACE

OXFORD
UNIVERSITY PRESS

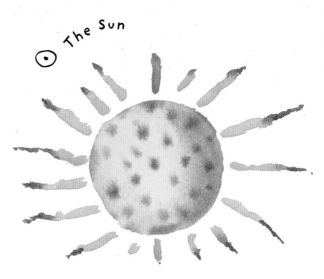

⊙ The Sun

Winnie the Witch loved to look through her telescope at the night sky.

It was huge and dark and mysterious. 'I'd love to go into space, Wilbur,' Winnie would say. 'It would be such a big adventure.'

Wilbur, Winnie's big black cat, loved to be outside at night too. He liked to chase moths and bats and shadows.

That was enough adventure for Wilbur.

☿ Mercury

Then one night, when the Moon and stars were bright, Winnie suddenly said, 'Let's go into space right now, Wilbur!'

'**Meeow?**' said Wilbur.

'But how will we get there?' wondered Winnie. 'We need a rocket, and I don't have a rocket.' Then she looked up at the Moon, and she had a wonderful idea.

She waved her magic wand, shouted,

'Abracadabra!'

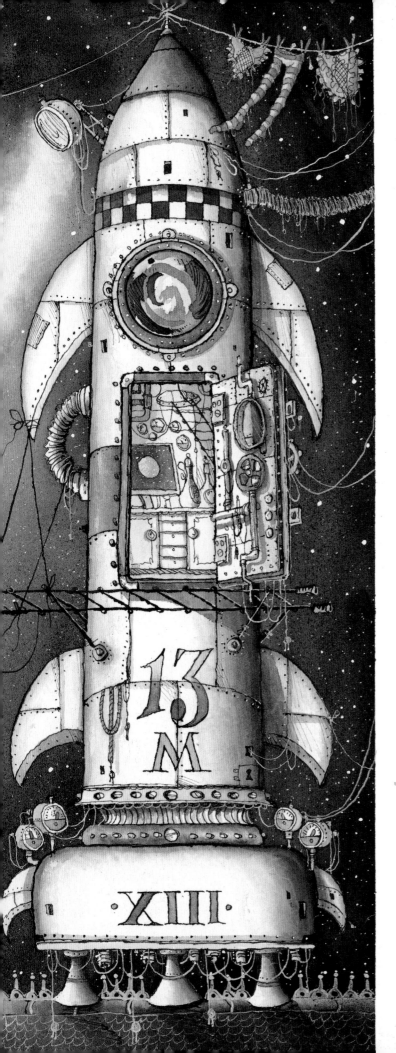

Venus

. . . and there, on the roof, was a rocket. Winnie packed a picnic basket, got her Big Book of Spells, just in case, and ran up the stairs with Wilbur.

Winnie shut her eyes, waved her magic wand, and shouted,

'Abracadabra!'

10
9
8
7
6
5
4 . . .

Earth

3
2
1 . . . .

The rocket shot off
the roof and into space.
It went very, very fast.
And it was hard to steer.

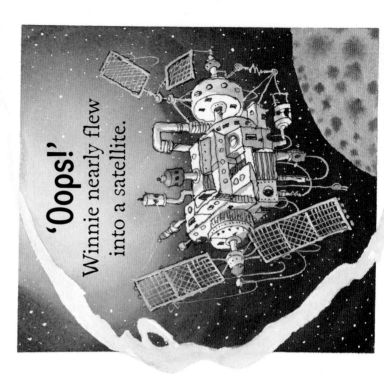

'Oops!'
Winnie nearly flew
into a satellite.

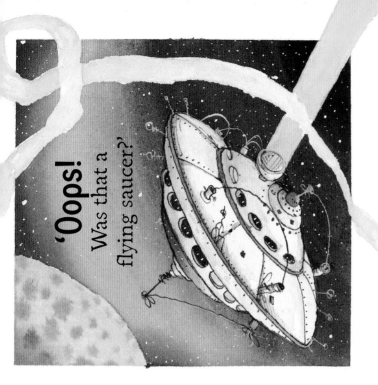

'Oops! Was that a flying saucer?'

'Oops! That was a falling star, Wilbur!'

WHOOSH!

The Moon

'**Meeow!**' said Wilbur.
He put his paws over his eyes.

'We'll find a lovely planet for our
picnic, Wilbur,' Winnie said.

Wilbur peeped out from
behind his paws. There were
little planets everywhere.

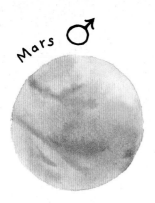

Mars ♂

'Here's a sweet little planet,' Winnie said. 'We'll have our picnic here.'

'**Purr!**' said Wilbur. He loved picnics.

PLOP! The rocket landed. All was quiet and peaceful. But there were funny little holes everywhere. Wilbur looked down the holes. They seemed to be empty . . .

Winnie unpacked the food. There were pumpkin scones, chocolate muffins, some cherries, and cream for Wilbur. **Yum!**

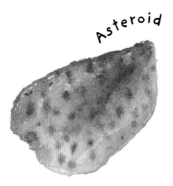

Asteroid

A little head popped out of a hole, and then there were heads everywhere.

'Rabbits!' said Winnie. 'Space rabbits are coming to our picnic!'

'Meeow!' said Wilbur.

A space rabbit hopped over to try some cream. **Yuck!**

Another space rabbit tried a pumpkin scone. **Horrible.**

Chocolate muffins? **Disgusting.** Cherries? **Yuck!**

Then some of the space rabbits hopped over to the rocket.

They sniffed it . . .

♃ Jupiter

and took a bite. Then the rocket was covered in space rabbits.

'Oh no!' shouted Winnie. She waved her magic wand, shouted, 'Abracadabra!'

and carrots and lettuces rained down on the rabbits. But the space rabbits didn't like carrots or lettuces.

'Of course!' said Winnie. She waved her magic wand, shouted,

'Abracadabra!'

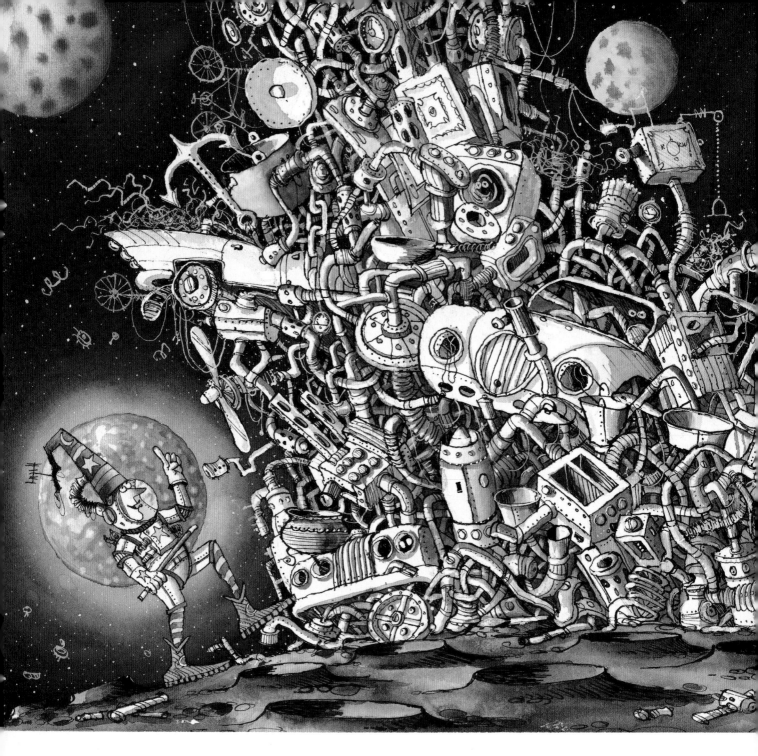

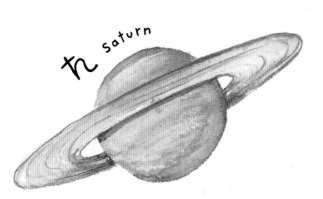

. . . and there was a giant
pile of metal.

Saucepans,
wheelbarrows,
bicycles,
cars,
even a fire engine.

Yes! That was what space rabbits liked.

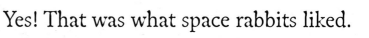

Scrumptious!
But it was too late . . .

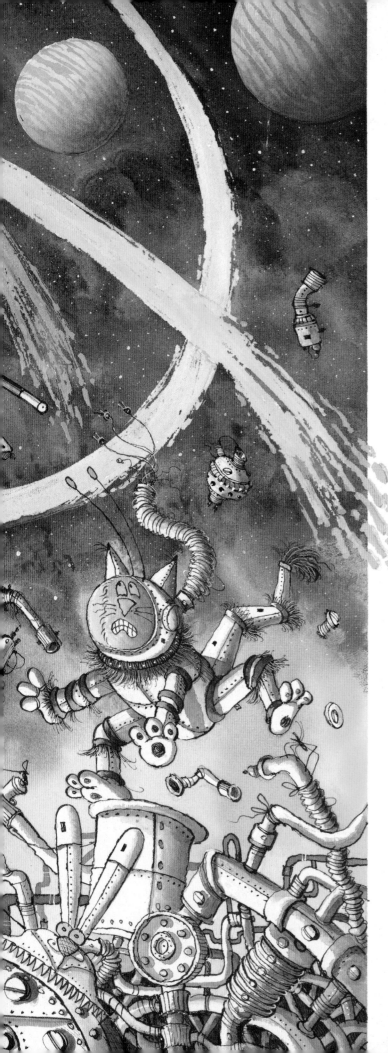

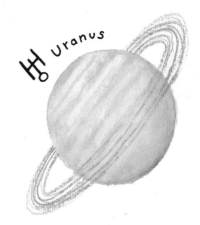

Uranus

the space rabbits had eaten up all of Winnie's metal rocket.

'Blithering broomsticks!' shouted Winnie. 'Now how will we get home?'

'Meeeow!' said Wilbur.

Winnie looked at the giant pile of metal. 'Perhaps,' she said. 'Maybe. I wonder.'

She looked in her Big Book of Spells. 'Yes!' she said.

Then she picked up her magic wand, waved it five times, and shouted,

'Abracadabra!'

There was a flash of fire, a bang . . .

Neptune

and there, on top of the giant
pile of metal, was a rattling,
roaring scrap metal rocket.

Winnie and Wilbur climbed
up to the rattling, roaring
rocket and jumped in.

vrOOM!
The rocket blasted away.
It rushed and roared
through space.

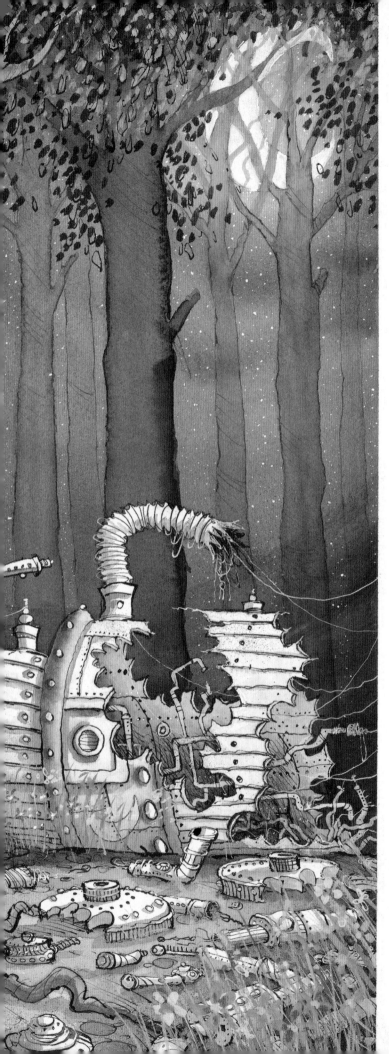

Pluto

WHUMP!

The rocket landed in Winnie's garden.

'That was an adventure, Wilbur,' Winnie said. 'But I'm glad we're home.'

'**P**urr, purr, purr,' said Wilbur.

He was very glad to be home.

Bethany

Katia

Eun-Jae

Kathleen

Ji-Eun

Jenny

Sara

Fraser

Ka Keung

Selin

Selin

Olivia

Siyabend

Kieran

A note for grown-ups

Oxford Owl is a FREE and easy-to-use website packed with support and advice about everything to do with reading.

Informative videos

Hints, tips and fun activities

Top tips from top writers for reading with your child

Help with choosing picture books

For this expert advice and much, much more about how children learn to read and how to keep them reading ...

LOOK
for Oxford Owl
www.oxfordowl.co.uk